BELLA FENELLA

written by Jenny Watt   illustrated by Begüm Manav

For more information about my books, please go to my website:

https://booksbyjennywatt.com

Bella Fenella

Written by Jenny Watt

Illustrated by Begüm Manav

ISBN 978-1-915128-16-4

For Fenella

For her 5th birthday, Grandma made Fenella a new dress.

Everyone thought she looked very nice.

"Angelic," said Mummy.

"Adorable," said Daddy.

"Bella Fenella!" said Mrs. Coppella.

For her 8th birthday, Fenella wanted to wear her dress again.

"You're too tall," said Mummy.

"Please!" said Fenella.

So Mummy let down the hem.

Everyone thought she looked very nice.

"Beautiful," said Grandma.

"Bewitching," said Granddad.

"Bella Fenella!" said Mrs. Coppella.

For her 12th birthday, Daddy bought her a new dress.

"Do you like it?" asked Daddy.

"Yes ... but it doesn't have any roses."

So Mummy bought a sewing machine.

Everyone thought she looked very nice.

"Cute," said Sally.

"Classy," said Max.

"Bella Fenella!" said Mrs. Coppella.

Before her 15th birthday, Mummy hid the dress.

But Fenella found it in the closet.

"It's too short to wear as a skirt," said Mummy.

"Can I wear it as a top?" asked Fenella.

So Mummy joined a sewing club and learned how to make straps.

Everyone thought she looked very nice.

"Delightful," said Auntie.

"Divine," said Uncle.

"Bella Fenella!" said Mrs. Coppella.

By her 18th birthday, the roses had faded.

"I'm sorry, Fenella, there's nothing more I can do," said Mummy.

So Fenella painted new roses and wore it as a scarf.

Everyone thought she looked very nice.

"Elegant," said Suzie.

"Exquisite," said Sam.

"Bella Fenella!" said Mrs. Coppella.

When she was 30, Fenella got married.

Everyone thought she looked very nice.

"Graceful," said her mother-in-law.

"Gorgeous," said her husband.

"Bella Fenella!" said Mrs. Coppella.

"Thank goodness, no more roses!" said Mummy.

Bella Fenella just smiled.

THE END

A Note from the Author

In case you were wondering, "Who is this mysterious Mrs Coppella, who keeps popping up in the book...?"

Mrs Coppella is a friend of the family, whose name just happens to rhyme with Fenella.

I believe that it is always more fun to read books out loud with other people. That is why I try to include a refrain which listeners can say (or shout!) as the story is being told.

So please join in and say **"Bella Fenella, said Mrs Coppella"** as you read this book!

More books by Jenny Watt

Available from your local Amazon website.
For more information about these and other books, please
go to **https://booksbyjennywatt.com**

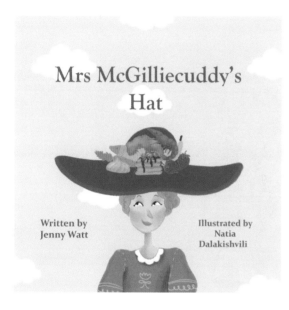

Mrs McGilliecuddy's Hat
Illustrated by Natia Dalakishvili

One day, Mrs McGilliecuddy buys a big blue hat. Her daughters, Isobel and Alice, suggest that she decorate it with their favourite foods. But when the hat is left on a park bench, they discover that they aren't the only ones who like bananas and pink meringues! Join Mrs McGilliecuddy and her daughters as they decorate the biggest blue hat in the world.
For ages 3 - 6 years

Yoo hoo, Mr Crab
Illustrated by Christine Cagara

Day after day, Mr. Crab enjoyed his quiet life. When the weather was good, he swam in the sea. In the evening, he listened to the waves as the sun set. But early one morning, he heard someone call... "Yoo hoo, Mr Crab!" And his life would never be the same again. This is the story of how Mr Crab became friends with a pretty blue crab named Lucy, who just wouldn't stop asking him to tea.
For ages 4 - 8 years

Printed in Great Britain
by Amazon

38551046R00016